GETTING ELECTED

The Diary of a Campaign

by Joan Hewett
photographs by Richard Hewett

LODESTAR BOOKS   E. P. DUTTON   NEW YORK

When I was growing up, politics seemed fascinating.
To Benjamin Bernstein, Carol Leeds, Merton Bernstein,
Boris Bogoslavsky, and Greta Lande, in fond remembrance.
J. H.

For Morris Hewett, who built my first darkroom.
And Will Connell and Eddy Kaminsky, who showed me how.
R. H.

Text copyright © 1989 by Joan Hewett
Photographs copyright © 1989 by Richard Hewett
All rights reserved.

Library of Congress Cataloging-in-Publication Data

Hewett, Joan.
  Getting elected: the diary of a campaign / by Joan Hewett;
photographs by Richard Hewett.—1st ed.
    p. cm.
  Bibliography: p.
  Includes index.
  Summary: Follows the political campaign of Gloria Molina
as she seeks election to the Los Angeles City Council.
    ISBN 0-525-67259-1
    1. City council members—California—Los Angeles—Juvenile
literature. 2. Elections—California—Los Angeles—Juvenile
literature. 3. Molina, Gloria. [1. City council members—
California—Los Angeles. 2. Elections—California—Los Angeles.
3. Molina, Gloria. 4. Politics, Practical.] I. Hewett, Richard,
ill. II. Title.
JS1005.A3H48 1988   88-11109
324.9794'94053—dc19   CIP
                                                        AC

Published in the United States by
E. P. Dutton, New York, N.Y.
a division of NAL Penguin Inc.

Published simultaneously in Canada by
Fitzhenry & Whiteside Limited, Toronto

Editor: Rosemary Brosnan   Designer: Barbara Powderly

Printed in the U.S.A.   W   First Edition
10 9 8 7 6 5 4 3 2 1

Gloria's election campaign is underway. Her spirits soar as she goes from door to door with her friend and coworker Robin.

"Flores is next," Robin says, as she checks the computer printout that lists the registered voters on the block. Gloria rings the doorbell. Her brown eyes sparkle as she talks.

"Good morning, Mrs. Flores. My name is Gloria Molina. I'm running for city council...."

Gloria is campaigning in Los Angeles' new political district. A special election has been called so the people in the district can choose their own city councilperson. Today is November 8. On February 3, voters will decide who that person will be.

Los Angeles is Gloria's hometown. She has spearheaded local Hispanic voter registration drives and fought for community day-care centers and other services. Now she is a member of the California State Assembly.

Some people who come to the door know Gloria by name and invite the two women in. They will size up the candidate for themselves!

Gloria answers their questions. She explains why she wants to be their city councilwoman and why she thinks that she would do an excellent job. And when people talk about the need for better housing or more police patrol units to cut down on crime, she listens closely.

While Gloria and Robin and other Molina for City Council teams canvass, aides at Molina for City Council headquarters gear for the long stretch.

Located on the second floor of a mini shopping mall, headquarters is close to a main freeway intersection and can be reached quickly from any part of the district. Banks of phones have been installed. A large refrigerator chest is packed with soft drinks, and the walls are beginning to be covered with campaign posters, political slogans, newspaper clippings, and notices.

Seated at rented desks or tables, volunteers answer phones, fold letters, stuff envelopes, and perform countless other tasks. Campaign signs are delivered. Alma Martinez, Gloria's campaign manager, tacks a large street map of the first district to the wall. The city council created this district so the people in this densely crowded area would have a councilperson to look after their interests. Because the district was drawn from surrounding ones, confusion over boundaries might occur. "If there's any doubt, check the map," Alma cautions.

Twenty-five-year-old Alma will be Gloria's "right hand" throughout the campaign. Basic strategy has been planned. Alma will carry it out. She is in charge of the whole staff. Her word will be final.

As in many city council elections, the candidates are not nominees of the Republican party, the Democratic party, or any political group. They run as individuals. To qualify for this race, a candidate must get 2,000 voters who live in the district to sign a petition that says they would like this person's name to be on the ballot.

Gloria entered the race early. She raised money and chose her staff. She was the first person to become an official candidate. Newspaper and TV reporters have been covering her campaign. Her get-out-in-front, stay-out-in-front strategy is working.

Now the end of November nears. An uneasy quiet hangs over headquarters. Although seventeen people have claimed that they would, no one else has officially entered the race. Then one person qualifies, and another. . . .

There will be four candidates for city council. At thirty-eight, Gloria is the oldest. She is the only woman.

To be elected, a candidate must receive 50 percent of the vote, plus one additional vote. If no one does, there will be a runoff in the spring between the two top vote-getters.

In a four-way race, can one person get more than half the vote? Gloria is sure that she can, and that is good enough for her loyal assistants. Like Alma, most of them are young and have gained experience working on other campaigns. They are proud to be on Gloria's team and are ready to give their all.

Aside from deciding who will do what, Alma writes Gloria's press releases and looks over all the information that goes out to be sure that it is correct and true to Gloria's views. She oversees Gloria's calendar and makes certain that heavy traffic and freeway routes have been considered so Gloria can get to her appointments on time. Alma also speaks to voters who are active in local community organizations. Will they support Gloria? Would they host an evening get-together or a "coffee" on a weekend and invite people who would like to meet Gloria? Like their hosts, these people would get out and vote and influence others to do the same.

Another assistant concentrates on recruiting volunteers. She calls unions and other groups that Gloria has helped in the past. A steady stream of volunteers—including walkers, telephoners, and drivers—will be needed from now through election day.

On weekends, volunteer walkers cheerfully troop into headquarters. Martha, another assistant, leads a training session. She smiles warmly and says, "Good morning. I want to thank you all for coming out for Gloria. One vote can make a difference. You can make that difference for us."

Although more than 200,000 people live in the first district, less than half that number are registered voters. The registered voters are the target; they are who the walkers will be seeing. Each team of walkers will have a campaign kit and a sheet that lists, block by block, the voters' names and addresses.

"Relax, be friendly," Martha coaches. "Tell people why you think Gloria is the best candidate. Then ask if she can count on their support."

Martha holds up a walking sheet for everyone to see. "Rate each voter. Circle *1* if the voter is for Gloria, *2* if the voter is undecided,

and *3* if the person is for another candidate. Write *N.H.* by the person's name if no one is home."

Now Martha talks about their vote-by-mail drive. "We're encouraging Gloria's supporters to vote by absentee ballot. You have forms requesting absentee ballots in your kits. Offer them to people who might find it hard to leave their homes. Wait while they fill out the forms, so you can mail them.

"Any questions? Okay. Pick a partner. Eat something before you go. Take an apple with you. Good luck!"

Walkers fan out. Most have to drive to reach their assigned precincts, which are subdivisions within a district. When the canvass is completed, assistants will feed the information into a computer, and the computer will tell them what percentage of the voters are for Gloria. They will also learn how her popularity differs from one community to another.

The district is actually a hodgepodge of separate communities, all of them old. The few well-to-do communities want to limit new housing, but most desperately need it. The area teems with recent immigrants. Many communities are predominantly Hispanic, and there are Asian neighborhoods also.

Gloria thinks that computers are a very useful campaign tool, but she does not rely on surveys to tell her what people think or feel. With an eye on the map, she picks a neighborhood and spends time there talking to the residents. As she goes from house to house, she gets a sense of what it would be like to live there. In one area, barred windows face the street and walls are scarred with graffiti. Not many blocks away, flowers brighten front-door paths.

It is mid-December and Gloria's supporters cannot stop smiling. There is a sweet, heady feeling that everything is going their way. Telephone callers have reached most of the "not at homes," and the results of the latest weekend canvass are in. Fifty-three percent of the voters support Gloria, 35 percent are undecided, and 12 percent are for someone else.

Gloria is delighted, but a trifle wary. The results are almost too good to be true.

While other candidates map their strategy and get out their first campaign literature, Gloria's volunteers ready their second mailing.

Christmas and New Year's Day come and go. Then the telephones at headquarters start to ring and ring.

Citizens' groups, political clubs, and other associations want to get the candidates together to debate. So do some local TV stations. Civic organizations invite Gloria to be their guest speaker. Neighborhood centers, including one for senior citizens, ask if Gloria will greet their members.

Newspaper reporters interview the candidates at length. This is important for the contenders. Reporters and editors will weigh what they say, decide who would make the best councilperson, and then their newspapers will endorse that person.

Many people think that a California State Assemblywoman is more important than a Los Angeles City Councilwoman. Reporters ask Gloria why she wants to go from two terms in the state assembly to the city council. Gloria explains that she is one out of eighty lawmakers in the assembly, but in the city council she would be one out of fifteen. Her opinions would count for more, and she hopes that she could help mold this growing, changing city and make it a better place for people to live.

Public debates, known as forums, are scheduled. At schools, community centers, and churches, auditoriums are packed with voters who are eager to learn more about the candidates. Sometimes there are questions that each candidate must answer in turn. Sometimes specific questions are fired at certain candidates. At the beginning or end of each forum, candidates usually get five to seven minutes to sum up their qualifications.

Gloria thinks and talks fast. She answers each question that is put to her in a direct manner. She never shapes her remarks to fit the audience, and she does not talk down to anyone.

There is no single big election issue. People ask questions about crime, neighborhood security, street cleaning, housing, and jobs for local residents. Although the candidates suggest a range of solutions, there are no sharp clashes among them. Voters struggle to reach a decision. Each contender seems energetic, intelligent, and well-meaning, but who would best champion their needs? Perhaps more than the other candidates, Gloria has proved that she has the will, courage, and ability to go against the odds and succeed. This is surprising for someone who was a quiet, eager-to-please, unassertive child.

Gloria spoke only Spanish when she started kindergarten. Although she liked school and her teachers helped and encouraged her, she was never more than an average student. In high school she wondered if cheerleading would be as much fun as it seemed. But she did not try out. She was the oldest of ten children and knew without being told that her place was at home helping her mom.

Sounding somewhat amazed, Gloria recalls her school days. "I wasn't interested in anything I was studying, and I certainly never believed that I would go on to achieve much as an adult. You see, the Anglo world wasn't quite real to me, and school belonged to that world. The Anglo world beyond school was a total mystery."

When Gloria got a secretarial job and became independent, her self-confidence blossomed. She went to community college at night and then took a volunteer job helping disturbed teenagers. They could barely read. Gloria wanted to find out why schools were not doing more to help them. She started attending school board meetings, and became more and more interested in community concerns. For a long time she worked behind the scenes to bring about change. Then people began to look to this young Chicana (Mexican American woman) as a leader.

When Gloria decided to run for the California State Assembly, she assumed that the city's powerful Chicano (Mexican American male) politicians would support her. They told her a woman had no chance and backed a man. Gloria decided to run anyway. She had worked in the ranks for women's rights. Now women's rights groups rallied and raised money to support her successful campaign.

Election campaigns are very costly. Money is needed for telephones, lights, office supplies, office equipment, voter lists, stamps, food, and staff salaries. It is needed to print flyers, stationery, posters, and other materials.

Now a longtime friend hosts a party for people who have contributed fifty dollars or more to Gloria's city council election campaign. Among the guests are many women's rights activists. Gloria gets there a little late. While her arrival is announced, she catches her breath in the vestibule.

Then she enters the living room, looks around at all the familiar, friendly faces, and says, "I want to thank you all for making this day, and for having made so many days, easier."

That weekend a law firm hosts a fund-raiser. A mariachi band plays, and a radiantly happy Gloria chats with guests.

Congressman Edward Royball addresses the crowd. He tells them that he was Los Angeles' first Chicano city councilman. Gloria was California's first Chicana state assemblywoman. He supported her then, and he supports her now. Then Gloria speaks. Dressed in dinner clothes, Ron Martinez, Gloria's husband, listens from the sidelines. A businessman with no active interest in politics, he simply enjoys being with her.

The applause ends. And Gloria and Ron head straight for a dinner dance hosted by other supporters.

Today is Monday, January 10. Michael Woo becomes the fifth city councilperson to endorse Gloria. To make policy and get laws passed, council members have to analyze issues, weigh choices, and be prepared to compromise so they can reach a general agreement. When council members endorse a candidate, they are saying to voters: This is a person we respect and would be happy to work with.

Last weekend's canvass shows that Gloria's lead has narrowed slightly. Because all the candidates are now campaigning vigorously,

this is not surprising. Gloria is concerned, but her optimism springs back as she matches wits with her opponents and meets a growing number of voters.

To win, Gloria will have to appeal to a wide variety of people. The largest percentage of the district's voters are Anglo, which means they are Americans of European descent. Other voters come from Mexico, El Salvador, Guatemala, Nicaragua, China, Taiwan, Vietnam, and the Philippines. Many of these voters are new citizens who hold to their traditional customs and values.

By midweek it seems as if the whole campaign is being telescoped into the last dozen days. Gloria is a guest at a luncheon honoring the city's first Hispanic police officers to reach the rank of captain. The chief of police praises the men for their achievement and says he expects that someday soon there will be a Hispanic assistant chief of police. "Why not chief?" Gloria calls out. The chief of police and others chuckle.

A cheer goes up at headquarters when *La Opinion*, the city's major Spanish-language newspaper, endorses Gloria. Then a couple of days later, the *Los Angeles Times* follows suit.

Now it is January 27. The election is one week away. Gloria rushes from an afternoon radio interview to a TV station for a half-hour televised debate. When she reaches the studio, her assistant looks for a telephone. She will find out what is going on at headquarters and get Gloria's messages. Meanwhile, Gloria enters the studio. She is the third candidate there, and moments later the fourth candidate joins them. They greet one another politely.

By 4:45 P.M. Gloria is walking a precinct. She stops for a hamburger and discovers that the short-order cook lives in the district and that he and his wife are voting for her!

There is a brief lull at headquarters, and then that evening's volunteers begin to arrive. By 6:00 P.M. the main room hums with activity as telephoners go down their lists calling one undecided voter after another, and mailers chat and sort the final campaign literature. By 9:30 P.M. the number of volunteers has dwindled. Alma and other members of the staff settle in. They must find out which precincts still have not been walked and which have a high rate of voters and should be walked again.

Suddenly Gloria's staff is jarred. They learn that voters will receive another candidate's campaign flyer in the morning mail, attacking Gloria's record in the state assembly.

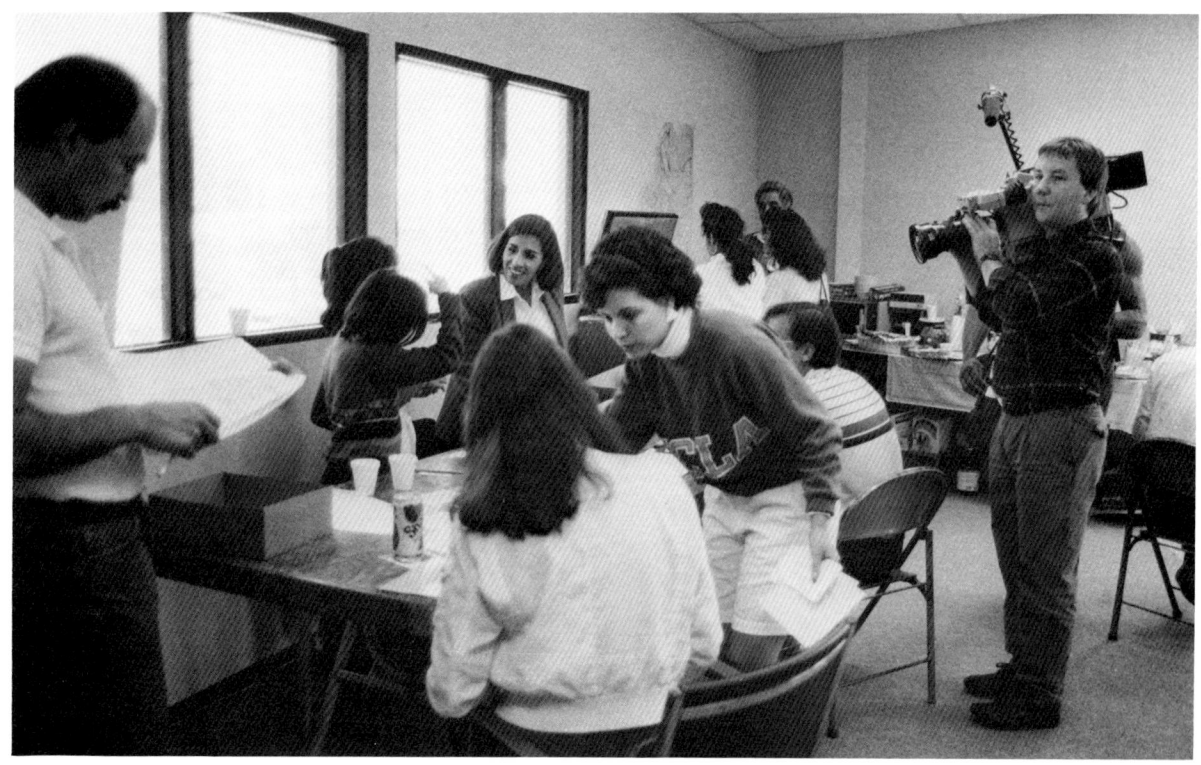

Gloria sees the flyer first thing in the morning and makes a decision. They will do a mass mailing and rebut the charges point by point. By 8:00 A.M. she is drafting a rebuttal.

On Saturday, headquarters is crammed with volunteers, and despite the last-minute attack, there is an upbeat, festive atmosphere. Some of the volunteers have been recruited; others are longtime Molina supporters or college and high school students who have been reading about the campaign. "If voters need rides to get to their polling places, be sure to get their phone numbers," an assistant tells the walkers.

By midmorning, Gloria's youngest sister, Olga, and a host of other telephoners are calling undecided voters. They remind them that Tuesday is election day and ask whom they are voting for.

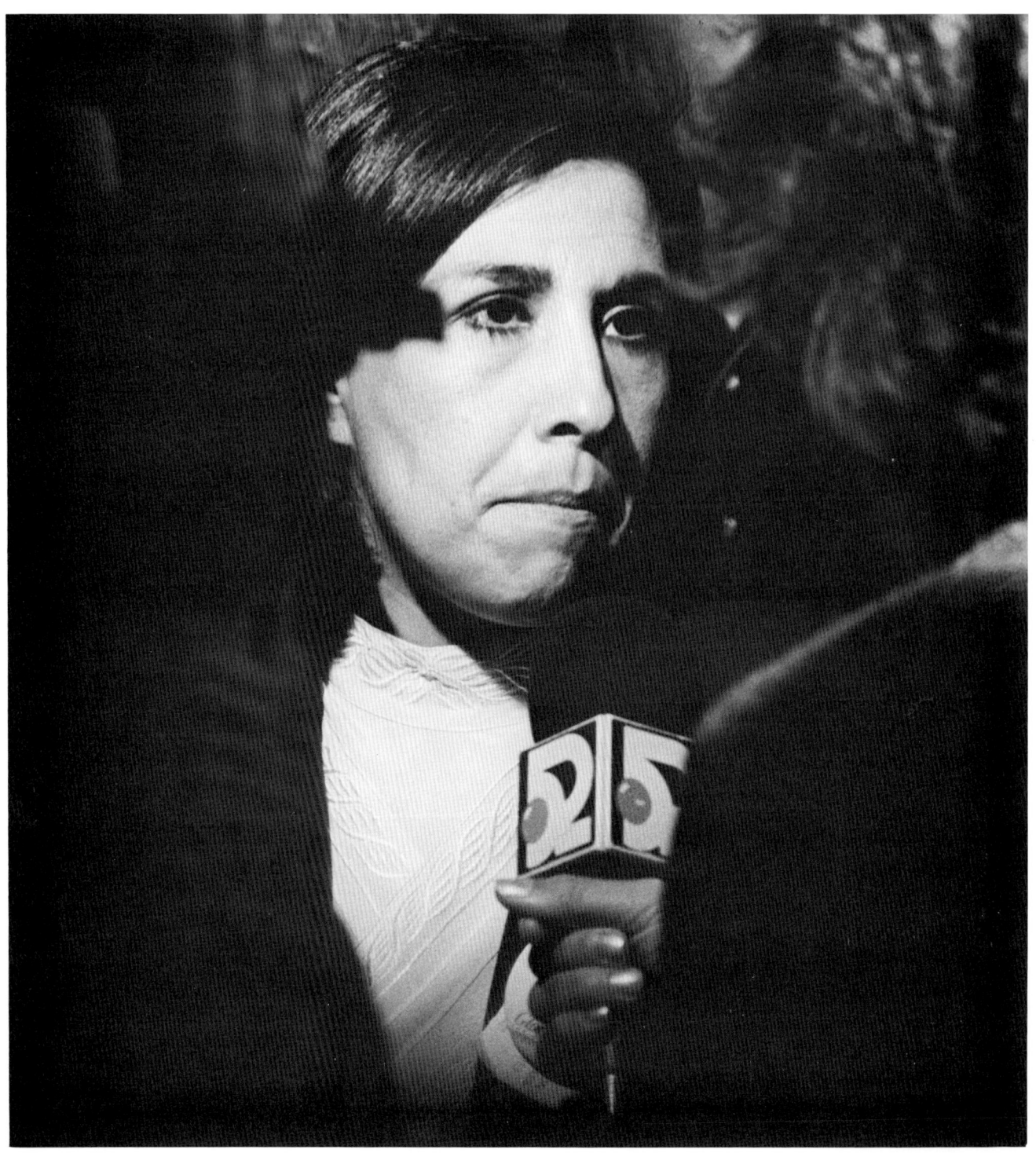

The volunteer turnout on Sunday is almost as large. One of Gloria's assistants says, "Volunteers are wonderful. They may not be familiar with all the issues, but their enthusiasm will often make up for it. In response to a question that they cannot answer, they may tell a voter about the time Gloria helped their Aunt Sadie cut through red tape to get medical aid. They are saying that Gloria cares, and the voter will remember that."

It is Monday, February 2. Most of the newspapers that have been predicting a Molina victory now say that the race is too close to call. One paper talks about a runoff in the spring. At headquarters, assistants go over their get-out-the-vote plans. By midafternoon, the results of the weekend telephone canvass are in, and the news is not encouraging. Gloria's spirits sink. Is the tide turning against her? She thinks of all the people who believed that she could win the first time around and worked so hard to make it happen, and the people who contributed as much money as they could and then gave more. Has she let them down?

A TV crew arrives. The reporter asks Gloria if she thinks she will get the needed vote. Gloria tells him it will be a close race, but she is sure she will win.

The afternoon rapidly darkens. Gloria decides that she should have a we'll-fight-in-the-spring-and-win speech ready. But she can't bring herself to write it. Not yet.

Election day arrives. At 4:30 A.M. a car pulls up in front of headquarters, and two figures dressed in jeans hop out. They unlock the door, dash into the office, and start making wake-up calls.

Walkers start arriving. By 5:00 A.M. flashlights, walking sheets, and door knockers—vote reminders—are given out. When the teams reach their assigned precincts, they split up to save time. Taking opposite sides of the street, they place door knockers on every Molina supporter's front door. Different precincts have different polling places. A sticker on each knocker gives the right address.

It is still dark. A skunk crosses a driveway. A dog howls. Some addresses are hard to see.

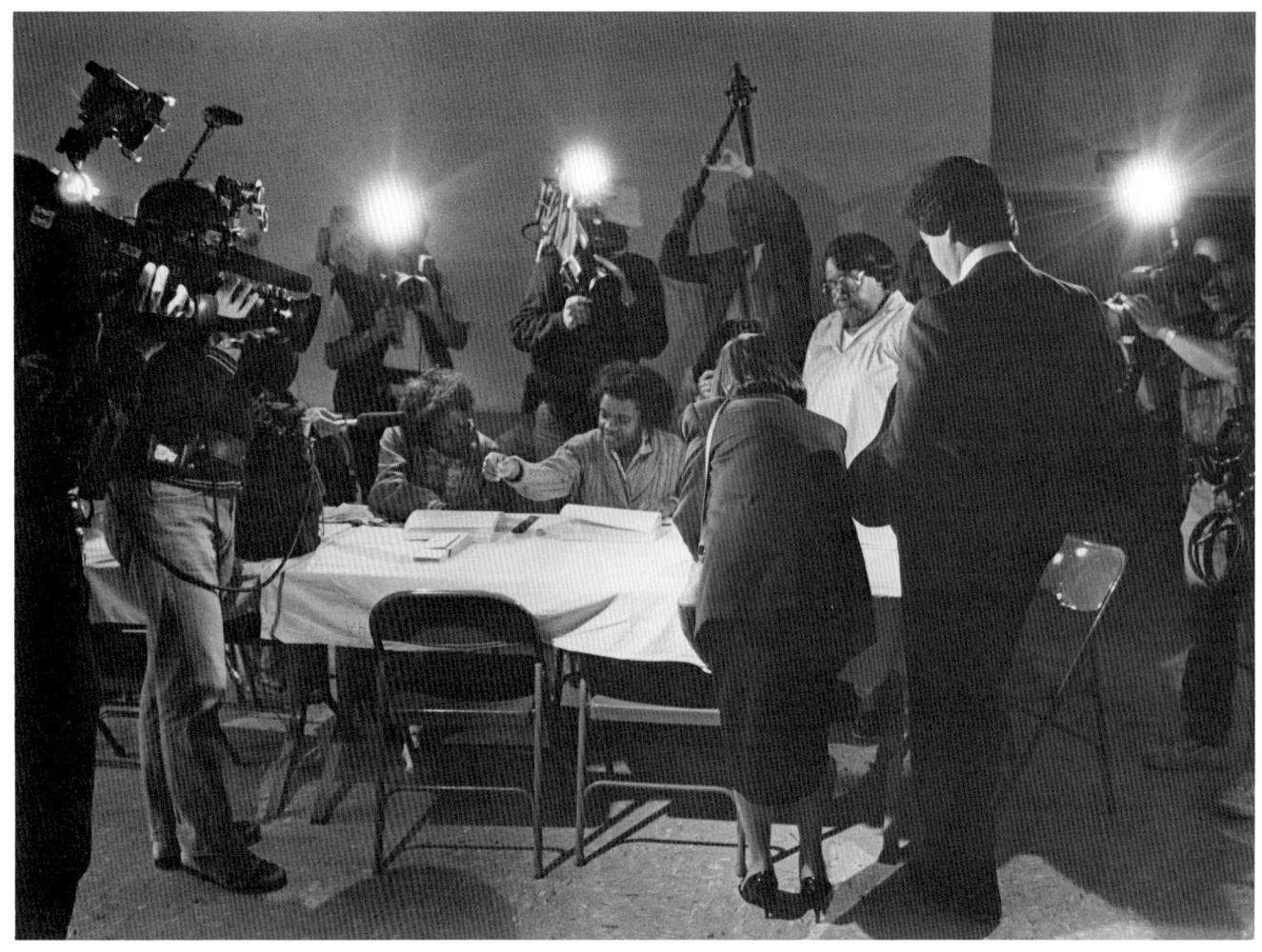

Headquarters stirs again at 6:30 A.M. as staff members make coffee and set out pencils and pads. From 7:00 A.M. when the polls open, to 8:00 P.M. when they close, an assistant will be by the phone to make sure that everyone who needs a ride to the polls gets one. Another assistant will be the poll watchers' contact.

Throughout the day, Gloria's poll watchers will go from polling place to polling place. At each one they will check their list of Gloria's supporters against the roster to find out who has still not voted, and they will call those names into headquarters. Then telephoners or walkers will try to reach those potential voters.

TV cameras roll as Gloria enters her polling place. Gloria votes, then cheerfully answers reporters' questions. She has slept late, feels much more confident, and for the first time in almost three months, has nothing pressing to do.

Two dozen determined telephoners stay glued to their phones. A busy signal is a good sign—someone is there! More and more supporters show up. Then newspaper reporters and TV news crews appear. Shifts of volunteers come and go. The room seems to bulge.

By 7:00 P.M. volunteers have campaign fever. In one neighborhood, a volunteer sees a voter getting out of a car carrying grocery bags. She follows the woman into her kitchen, convinces her that dinner can wait, escorts her back to her car, and points her in the right direction.

The polls close. Supporters make their way to a nearby recreation center to await the election returns. Dining tables have been set up in the gym. A buffet table is laden with food, and a dance band plays.

Gloria and her closest supporters gather in the adjoining office. They wait tensely for the desk telephone to ring. Only two people have been given the phone number, and they are at City Hall in a room where the final computer reading of the counted ballots takes place. First the absentee ballot count is computed. The results flash on an overhead TV monitor.

Moments later the phone rings. Gloria is stunned. Is it possible? She has received 61 percent of the absentee vote!

Alma goes out to break the news. The band stops playing, the room quiets, and when Alma finishes speaking the crowd goes wild.

Reports from different precincts come in. Gloria is clearly in the lead. Then at 9:35 P.M., the final tally is announced. Gloria has received 57 percent of the vote. She has won by a far wider margin than anyone expected or thought possible.

Now, as Gloria moves toward the gym stage, the crowd parts. There is a rhythmic stomping. "Glo-ree-ah, Glo-ree-ah," the chant rises and swells.

Gloria, her eyes bright with tears, addresses the now hushed crowd. "This is a victory for all of us. . . ."

FURTHER READING

Archer, Jules. *Winners and Losers: How Elections Work in America.* New York: Harcourt Brace Jovanovich, 1984.

Gray, Lee Learner. *How We Choose a President.* New York: St. Martin's Press, 1972.

Levenson, Dorothy. *Politics: How to Get Involved.* New York: Franklin Watts, 1980.

Lindop, Edmund. *The First Book of Elections.* New York: Franklin Watts, 1968.

Schwartz, Alvin. *The People's Choice: The Story of Candidates, Campaigns, and Elections.* New York: E. P. Dutton, 1968.

INDEX

ballots:
   absentee, 15, 43
   counting, 43, 44

California State Assembly, 6, 26
   Gloria's campaign for, 24
   Gloria's record in, 32
   Los Angeles City Council compared with, 20
   number of members in, 20
candidates, 10, 11
   campaigning by, 28–29, 32–34
   in debates, 19, 21
   endorsed by council members, 28
   newspaper interviews of, 20
   voters' needs and, 22
canvassing, canvassers (walkers), 4–8, 13, 14–16, 32, 34, 37, 41
   computer results of, 16
   on election day, 38
   by Gloria, 4–8
   voters rated by, 14–15
Chicano politicians, 24, 26
city council elections, 10
City Hall, 43
contributors, party for, 24–25

debates, public (forums), 19, 21, 31
door knockers, 38

election campaigns, money for, 24
election day, 6, 38–44
election returns, 43

forums (public debates), 19, 21, 31
fund-raiser, 25–26

Hispanic communities, 6, 16
Hispanic police officers, 30
Hispanic politicians, 24, 26

La Opinion, 30
Los Angeles, 6
   new political district of, 6, 9, 16
Los Angeles City Council, 6, 26
   California State Assembly compared with, 20
   candidates endorsed by members of, 28
   new district created by, 6, 9, 16
   number of members in, 20
Los Angeles City Council elections, 10
   candidates in, *see* candidates
   final tally in, 44
   issues in, 22
   percent of vote needed to win, 11
   predictions about, 37
Los Angeles Times, 30

mailings, 19, 34
Martinez, Alma, 9, 11–13, 43
Martinez, Ron, 26
Molina, Gloria:
   in California State Assembly, 6, 24, 32
   campaign flyer against, 32–34
   campaign manager of, 9
   candidacy of, reason for, 20

Molina, Gloria *(continued)*
   canvassing by, 4–8, 31
   as Chicana, 22–23, 26
   community work of, 6, 23
   in debates, 21, 31
   fund-raiser for, 25–26
   husband of, 26
   at police officer luncheon, 30
   school days of, 22–23
   strategy of, 9, 10
   volunteer job of, 23
   women's rights and, 24
Molina, Olga, 34
Molina for City Council headquarters, 8–9, 11, 31, 32
   on election day, 40
   student workers at, 34
   volunteers at, 8, 32, 34, 37

newspapers, 10, 41
   endorsement by, 20
   Gloria endorsed by, 30
   predictions made by, 37

party for contributors, 24–25
petitions, 10
police officers, 30
political parties, 10
polls, 40–41, 43
   precincts and, 38
poll watchers, 40
precincts, 16, 38, 44
press releases, 12

public debates (forums), 19, 21, 31

Royball, Edward, 26
runoff, 11, 37

telephone callers, 8, 13, 18, 19, 32, 34, 37, 41
television coverage, 10, 37
   of debates, 19, 31
   on election day, 41

volunteer(s), 8, 19, 32, 34, 41
   enthusiasm of, 37, 41
   recruiting, 13, 34
   walkers, 14; *see also* canvassing, canvassers
vote-by-mail drive, 15
vote reminders, 38
voters, 4, 6, 14
   in community organizations, 12–13
   ethnic backgrounds of, 29
   needs of, 6, 22
   petition signed by, 10
   poll watchers and, 40–41
   rating, 14–15
   rides for, 34, 40

walking, *see* canvassing, canvassers
women's rights, 24
Woo, Michael, 28